To Catherine:
With much love to you,
Aunt Ann, Uncle Jay,
Emily + Charlie
xoxo

Christmas 1992.

Rosie
and the Pavement Bears

Susie Jenkin-Pearce

HUTCHINSON
London   Sydney   Auckland   Johannesburg

Rosie was very small, the smallest in her class. And being small was not always fun…

…especially when Ben and Billy were around. Ben and Billy were BULLIES. They pushed Rosie when Mrs Partridge wasn't looking, they pulled her hair and stuck out their tongues.

They teased her on the way home.

'I shouldn't tread on the cracks if I were you!' jeered Billy.

'Nah!' sneered Ben. 'The bears'll get you.'

'Don't care,' sniffed Rosie. 'I'm not scared.' And she stepped on the cracks on purpose.

I wish the bears *would* come, thought Rosie. They can't be worse than Billy and Ben. So...

Rosie stepped on the cracks on the way to school.

She stepped on the cracks all the way home.

She stepped on the cracks
on the way to the park.
AND . . .
not one bear,
not a paw,
not a whisker.

Then one morning, as Rosie
walked to school, the thought of
those big bullies was more than
she could stand.

'It's not FAIR!' she shouted. 'Why don't they leave me alone?' and she stamped her foot down so hard that she bit her tongue and burst into tears.

'YAZOO!'
'BAZAM!'
came two gravelly voices. 'If you'd done that before,
we'd have been here sooner.'

'What, bitten my tongue?' said Rosie.

'No, silly,' said the two huge bears. 'Stamped on the
cracks, not tip-toed.'

Rosie felt good as she marched through the school gates. With two big bears beside her, she'd have no problems.

In class, Rosie knew all the answers.

For sums, she had her fingers *and* two sets of paws to count on.

In writing, her work looked much neater when *she* wasn't being pushed.

In PE she jumped higher than anyone in the class ever had before. Ben and Billy didn't do too well at all.

Then at lunchtime, the two bullies did some extremely silly things. Mr Robin was very cross. Suddenly Ben and Billy seemed rather stupid.

At storytime Rosie amazed everyone by
telling the best bear stories they had ever
heard. She had lots of great ideas.

Going home, Rosie felt happier than she had ever
felt before.

But as she rounded the corner of her street, she was horrified to see two big girls blocking the way of a small boy.

Rosie bristled with anger.
'Go on, Rosie,' said the bears. 'Get 'em!'

Rosie took a deep breath. 'How DARE you!' she
roared. 'Pick on someone your own size.'

The two big girls looked at Rosie in surprise.
Suddenly they were afraid. She had the look of an
angry bear.

Rosie took the little boy's hand.

'No need to be afraid,'
said Rosie. 'Not with the
Pavement Bears to help
us.'

But when she looked round, the Pavement Bears had gone.

'Yazoo! Bazam!' sang
Rosie, and they jumped
on the cracks all the way
home.

For Rosie The Invincible, the bravest bear of all.

*First published in 1991
Reprinted in 1991 by Hutchinson Children's Books
an imprint of the Random Century Group Ltd
20 Vauxhall Bridge Road, London SW1V 2SA*

*Random Century Australia (Pty) Ltd
20 Alfred Street, Milsons Point, Sydney, NSW 2061 Australia*

*Random Century New Zealand Ltd
PO Box 40-086, Glenfield, Auckland 10, New Zealand*

*Random Century South Africa (Pty) Ltd
PO Box 337, Bergvlei, 2012, South Africa*

Designed by Paul Welti

*Printed and bound in Belgium
by Proost International Book Production*

British Library Cataloguing in Publication Data is available

ISBN 0-09-174164-5